Andrea Ballance

Grasya Oliyko

CREATURE

Flying Eye Books

London | Los Angeles

My eyes open and close dreamily,
reflecting the whole universe.

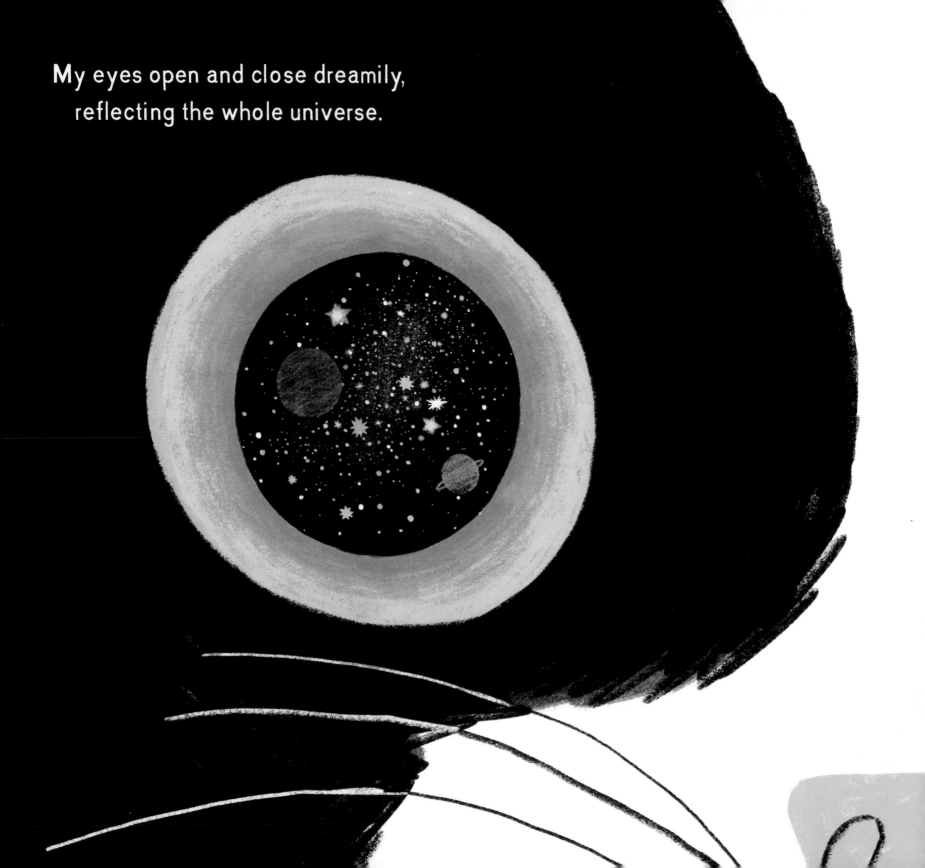

BETTWS

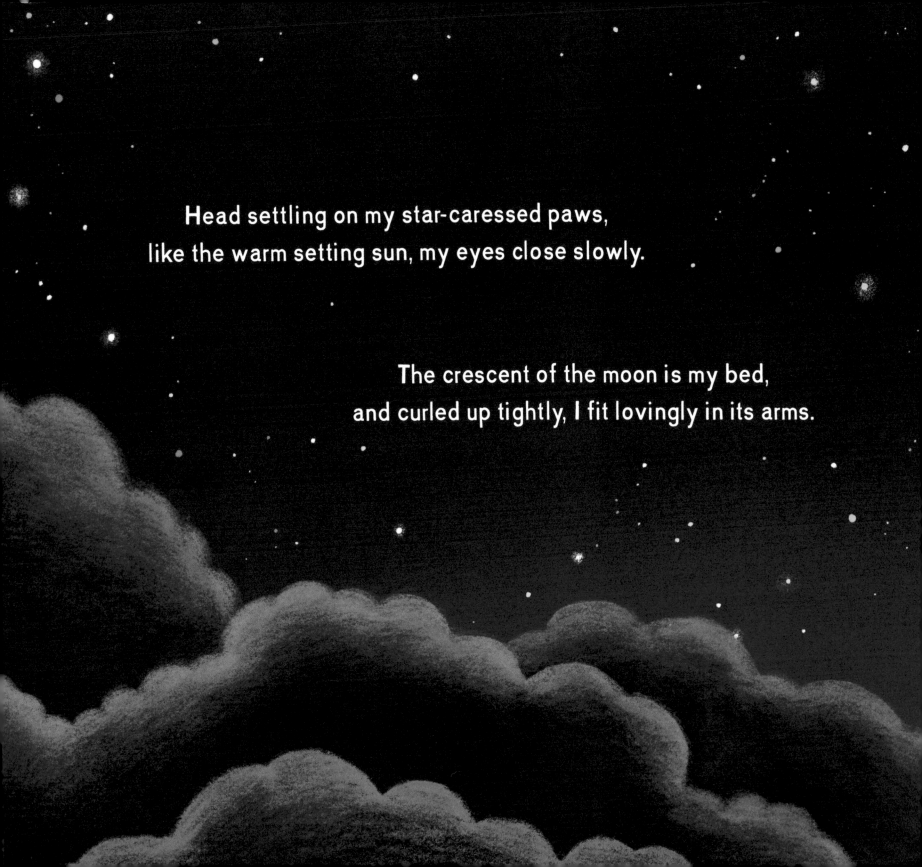

Head settling on my star-caressed paws,
like the warm setting sun, my eyes close slowly.

The crescent of the moon is my bed,
and curled up tightly, I fit lovingly in its arms.

until gravity's force
pulls me under,

ready for other-worldly
dreams to take hold.

Home again,
        I knead my heavenly bed

I drink deeply from the **Milky Way**,
my tummy expanding like space itself.

My attention is fully caught in this game for a while,
until I come back down to Earth.

– limitless,
expansive, infinite.

Like a rocket at rest, I catch my breath.
Ears back, eyes darting,
adventure is everywhere –

No obstacles stand in my way,
as I scale the great gas giants with ease.

In the chaos I fly!
Sliding and skidding into stars.

causing worlds to be born
in the big bangs I create.

I send everything hurtling,
diverted to new parts of the universe,

Like a supernova I am ready to...

Startled, I stop ... still.

Asteroids and comets shoot past me,

as I dissolve into the blackness of space.

This magnificent expanse is my home,
and it gets my divine approval.

Eyes wide open, I see everything.
I am elegant but deadly.

Happy and blissful,

rubbing my sleek body
through its fingers.

Craving adoration and love,

I weave in and out
of the pillars of creation.

as I lick my paws and wipe
cosmic dust from my whiskers.

I am radiant, energised,
prepared for lift-off!

My body vibrates
with contented purrs,

Reaching out, then curling my paws back in,
I watch as the fabric of space swirls around them

I stretch out, roll over and yawn,

exposing my furry tummy like
a solar system.

Small, sparkling stars twinkle here and there,
each iris awakening, flaring with golden solar light.

To Flying Eye Books. To all my family.
To Dan and my children, They and He. Keep being
your authentic, neurodivergent selves.

-A.B.

To my grannies and grandpas.
To all stray cats and dogs, who definitely
deserve to have homes and loving families.

-G.O.

First edition published in 2021 by Flying Eye Books,
an imprint of Nobrow Ltd. 27 Westgate Street, London, E8 3RL.

1 3 5 7 9 10 8 6 4 2

Published in the US by Nobrow (US) Inc.
Printed in Poland on FSC® certified paper.

ISBN: 978-1-83874-041-2
www.flyingeyebooks.com